Karen's Big Lie

Look for these
and other books about Karen
in the
Baby-sitters Little Sister series:

Little Sister

Karen's Big Lie
Ann M. Martin

Illustrations by Susan Tang

A
LITTLE APPLE
PAPERBACK

SCHOLASTIC INC.
New York Toronto London Auckland Sydney

No part of this publication may be reproduced in whole or in part, or stored in a retrieval system, or transmitted in any form or by any means, electronic, mechanical, photocopying, recording, or otherwise, without written permission of the publisher. For information regarding permission, write to Scholastic Inc., 730 Broadway, New York, NY 10003.

ISBN 0-590-45655-5

Copyright © 1993 by Ann M. Martin. All rights reserved. Published by Scholastic Inc. APPLE PAPERBACKS and BABY-SITTERS LITTLE SISTER are registered trademarks of Scholastic Inc.

12 11 10 9 8 7 6 5 4 3 2 1   3 4 5 6 7 8/9

Printed in the U.S.A.   40

First Scholastic printing, May 1993

This book is for
Godwin Agbeli
and my friends in Kopeyia

Karen's School

I was in school. I was having a little trouble paying attention. That happens sometimes, even though I like my teacher very much. My teacher's name is Ms. Colman, and she is gigundoly wonderful. She is my best, best teacher ever. She likes me, too. She is getting married soon, and I am going to be the flower girl in her wedding.

Ms. Colman was standing at the chalkboard. She was writing numbers on it. Math is not my favorite subject. It is a little hard for me. I am better at reading and writing and science.

It was a Friday afternoon. I was thinking about the weekend. I was thinking about the warm weather, too. In the courtyard outside our classroom, flowers were blooming. Bees were buzzing back and forth. A yellow butterfly zipped by.

Next to me, Ricky Torres was scribbling numbers on a piece of paper. Ricky just loves math. I will never know why. Guess what. Ricky is my husband. (Well, he is my pretend husband.) We got married on the playground one day.

I am Karen Brewer, Ricky's wife. I have blonde hair and blue eyes and some freckles. I wear glasses. So does Ricky. That is why we sit next to each other. Ms. Colman makes the glasses-wearers sit in the front row. I guess she is allowed to do that. She wears glasses herself. Also, she is the teacher.

I am seven. Ricky is almost eight. So are

most of the kids in our second-grade room. In fact, some of them have already turned eight. I am the youngest in the class. That is because I skipped.

Ms. Colman had picked up a stack of papers. She was standing at her desk. "Class," she began, "today you are going to take a math quiz. So are the other students here at Stoneybrook Academy. Everyone is going to begin taking quizzes about the things they have studied in math this year. Our quizzes will be on addition and subtraction facts. Those facts will be helpful when you learn to multiply and divide. I will give you a quiz once or twice a week, but I will not tell you about them ahead of time. Just begin reviewing your facts. Use the flash cards you got at the beginning of the year. And do not worry too much about this first quiz, since it is a surprise."

Ms. Colman handed out the papers. I looked down at the one on my desk. I saw two long columns of addition problems, like this: $9 + 8 = \underline{\hspace{1cm}}$. $7 + 11 = \underline{\hspace{1cm}}$.

"Boo," I whispered.

Then Ms. Colman said, "Oh, one more thing. The quizzes will be timed. When I say, 'Time's up,' you must stop working. Even if you have not finished. Is that clear?"

Well, bullfrogs. This was getting worse and worse.

"Okay," said Ms. Colman, looking at her watch. "You may begin."

I picked up my pencil. I counted on my fingers. I answered the first question. Next to me, Ricky was writing away. He filled in one answer after another. He does not count on his fingers. He used to, but not anymore. I answered another question. I looked at Ms. Colman. She was busy erasing the chalkboard. When she had finished, she tacked some things to the bulletin board.

"Time's up," she said a few minutes later.

Already? I dropped my pencil. I was not finished. I had skipped a lot of the problems. It is hard to concentrate on a Friday afternoon.

Karen's Families

On Fridays, I think about the weekend. I like weekends. Mine are usually interesting. Guess what. I have two families. Every other weekend I go to Daddy's house. In between, I live at Mommy's house. This is because my mommy and daddy do not live together. They are divorced.

When I was little, I lived in one house with my mommy, my daddy, and my brother Andrew. (Andrew is four now, going on five.) It was a big house. I was very happy. But Mommy and Daddy were not. They began to fight. Finally they told Andrew and me about the divorce. After the divorce, Mommy moved into a little house, and Daddy stayed in the big house. (That is the house he grew up in. Both houses are here in Stoneybrook, Connecticut.) Mommy took Andrew and me with her.

After awhile, Mommy and Daddy both got married again. But not to each other. Mommy married a man named Seth. He is my stepfather. Daddy married a woman named Elizabeth. She is my stepmother. Most of the time, Andrew and I live with Mommy and Seth. But every other weekend, and on some holidays and vacations, we live at Daddy's big house.

Here's who lives at the little house: Mommy, Seth, Andrew, me, Rocky, Midgie, and Emily Junior. Rocky and Midgie are Seth's cat and dog. Emily Junior is my pet rat.

It is lucky Daddy's house is so big, because here is who lives in it: Daddy, Elizabeth, Andrew, me, Nannie, Kristy, Charlie, Sam, David Michael, Emily Michelle, Shannon, Boo-Boo, Goldfishie, and Crystal Light the Second.

You see, Elizabeth was married once before she married Daddy. Kristy, Charlie, Sam, and David Michael are her kids. (They are my stepsister and stepbrothers.) Kristy is thirteen. She baby-sits. I just love her. She is the best big sister. Charlie and Sam go to high school. David Michael is seven, like me. (But he does not go to my school.) Emily Michelle is my adopted sister. Daddy and Elizabeth adopted her from a faraway country called Vietnam. Emily is two and a half. (I named my rat after her.) Nannie is Elizabeth's mother, so she is my stepgrandmother. She helps take care of us kids.

Okay, on to the pets. Shannon is David Michael's puppy. (She is *big* for a puppy.) Boo-Boo is Daddy's cross old tomcat. And Goldfishie and Crystal Light are fish. They belong to Andrew and me.

I have nicknames for my brother and me. I call us Andrew Two-Two and Karen Two-Two. (I got the idea from a book Ms. Colman read to our class. It was called *Jacob Two-Two Meets the Hooded Fang*.) These are good names for us because we have two houses and two families, two mommies and two daddies, two cats and two dogs — and two of lots of other things. I have two pairs of sneakers, one at each house. I have two stuffed cats. Moosie stays at the big house, Goosie stays at the little house. I even have two pieces of Tickly, my special blanket. Plus, Andrew and I have clothes and books and toys at each house. That way, we do not have to pack much when we go back and forth.

Guess what else I have two of. I have two best friends. Hannie Papadakis lives across the street from Daddy and one house down. Nancy Dawes lives next door to Mommy. Hannie and Nancy are in Ms. Colman's class, too. We call ourselves the Three Musketeers.

Sometimes being a two-two is hard, but mostly it is okay. On the day of the math quiz, I did not mind it. I was looking forward to a big-house weekend.

David Michael

The weekend at Daddy's got off to a good start. On Friday night, everyone in my big-house family was at home, so we ate dinner together. We ate in the backyard on picnic tables. Daddy and Kristy barbecued chicken. When dinner was over, Elizabeth said, "What shall we have for dessert?"

And right then, we heard the jingling of bells. Mr. Tastee's truck was driving slowly down the street.

"Ice cream!" I cried.

And Andrew added, "I scream, you

scream, we all scream for ice cream!"

Everyone bought an ice cream from Mr. Tastee. Even Nannie.

On Saturday, Hannie came over. We worked in the vegetable garden that Daddy plants every year. (We are hoping for a good crop of pumpkins for Halloween.) Later, Kristy took us to the playground. We came back late in the afternoon, and Hannie had to go home.

Kristy and I wandered into the backyard at the big house. The rest of the family was there. Even Sam and Charlie, who are usually off with their friends. Charlie had just made a pitcher of iced tea.

"Hi!" Emily Michelle called to us.

"Come sit down," added Elizabeth.

Kristy and I squished together in a lawn chair. I just love being with my whole, entire big-house family. I looked around at them. Elizabeth was mending a shirt. Nannie was reading the paper. Daddy was checking the vegetable garden. Andrew and Emily were looking for lady-

12

bugs. Charlie and Sam were serving the iced tea.

David Michael was not doing a thing. He was just sitting on the ground. All of a sudden he said, "Mom? Can I get a buzzsaw?"

"Excuse me?" said Elizabeth.

Daddy left the garden. "Need some tools?" he asked.

"No!" howled David Michael. "A buzzsaw. I want a buzzsaw. It's a haircut. All the guys in school are getting buzzsaws."

"They shave the sides of their heads," spoke up Sam.

"Oh," said Elizabeth. "Then, no, you may not get a buzzsaw."

"But my friends have them!" said David Michael.

"You are not your friends," replied Elizabeth.

"Please?"

"Absolutely not."

"Could I get one of my ears pierced?" asked David Michael.

"No," said Elizabeth and Daddy at the same time.

"How about a tattoo?"

"Out of the question," said Daddy.

"I'll say," agreed Elizabeth.

"My friends think I am a baby," wailed David Michael. "I am not cool."

"Do you know how you *get* a tattoo?" asked Sam. "First you go to a tattoo parlor. Then a guy pricks you over and over again with a big needle. That is how he draws the design. With needles."

"Ew," I said.

"What is a tattoo parlor?" asked Andrew.

"Never you mind," said Nannie.

And Elizabeth added, "So no pierced ear, no tattoos, and no buzzsaws, young man. Do you understand?"

"Yes," replied David Michael. But right after dinner that night, he pulled me aside. "Karen," he said, "I have decided to get a tattoo."

"Don't do it," I exclaimed, but I knew he would not listen to me.

14

The Red 68

It was Monday. The big-house weekend was over. Andrew and I had gone back to the little house, and now I was in school again. When reading was over, Ms. Colman said, "Please put away your workbooks, girls and boys. Clear your desks."

Ms. Colman was standing at the front of the room. She was holding a stack of papers.

Ricky leaned over. He poked me with the eraser end of his pencil. "I think those are our quizzes," he whispered.

I nodded. I was not worried.

Ms. Colman walked up and down the rows. She handed our quizzes back to us. I could see red marks on the papers. Finally she gave me mine. I looked at it. On the top was a red 68.

A 68! That was awful! Well, it was awful for me. In most subjects I get 90s or even 100s. And in math I usually get 80s, and *sometimes* 90s. But a 68. How had that happened?

I put my hand over the top of my paper to cover up the 68. Then I glanced at Ricky's paper. Ricky was not covering his. That was because he had gotten an 88.

Bullfrogs. Well, we had not known about the quiz. Maybe that was why I had gotten a 68. I probably would have done better if I had studied. Plus, the quiz was timed. How could anyone solve all those problems so fast? I had not had enough time to count on my fingers. I would just have to study. That was all. As soon as I got home that afternoon, I would look for my flash cards.

They were around somewhere. (Unless they were at the big house. I do not have two boxes of flash cards.)

"Class," said Ms. Colman. She had finished handing back the papers. She was standing by her desk. "Some of you may not be happy with your scores. Do not worry too much. You need to get used to taking timed quizzes. You also need to memorize your addition and subtraction facts. You should get to know them so you can answer them like *that*." (Ms. Colman snapped her fingers.) "So find your flash cards and start quizzing yourselves. And for those of you who did well on Friday's quiz — congratulations. Keep up the good work. We will have another quiz soon."

On the playground that day, Hannie and Nancy and I climbed to the top of the monkey bars.

"Boy," I said, "our addition quiz was hard."

"Yeah," agreed my friends.

18

"Extra hard," added Nancy. "I only got a seventy-six."

"Seventy-six!" I cried. "Boy."

"What did you get?" Nancy asked me.

"A sixty-eight," I replied. "A big red sixty-eight."

"Karen, you never get sixties," said Hannie.

"I know. What did you get?"

"A ninety-three," Hannie replied.

"Wow," said Nancy and I. (Well, Hannie's best subject *is* math.)

"Ricky got an eighty-eight," I went on. "He did not count on his fingers."

"Did you count on your fingers?" Hannie asked.

"Yes. I always do."

"You should memorize the facts," said Hannie. (She sounded like Ms. Colman.) "Counting is too slow."

"But it works," I replied. "Oh, well, I will just have to look at the flash cards. Then I will do better. Come on. Let's play hopscotch."

The Next Test

When I returned home after school that day, I was ready to study. I was ready to memorize my addition and subtraction facts.

"Mommy?" I said. "Do you know where my flash cards are?"

"What flash cards?" she replied.

"The ones Ms. Colman gave us at the beginning of the year. For math." (The beginning of the year seemed like a very long time ago.)

"Are they in your desk?" suggested Mommy.

The flash cards were not in my desk. I looked in every drawer. Then I searched my room. No flash cards. I called the big house and asked Kristy to search my room there. No flash cards. I looked in the playroom. Finally I found the flash cards in Andrew's toy chest. I decided I was too tired to study them. I would study them the next day. At least I had found them.

On Tuesday I did study. A little. I sat on the floor in my room. The box of flash cards was in front of me. Emily Junior was in my lap. I looked at a couple of the cards. Then I played with Emily. I looked at another card. I played with Emily some more. I really did not study too much.

On Wednesday I did not study at all.

On Thursday Ms. Colman gave us another quiz.

Uh-oh.

That was pretty sneaky. The first quiz

had been on Friday. I was not expecting the next quiz to be on Thursday. I had planned to study on Thursday after school. Boo and bullfrogs.

Ms. Colman stood before us. She was holding the papers. "The quiz will be the same as before," she said. "These are addition problems. I will time you, so work as quickly as you can. When I say 'Time's up,' please put your pencils down. And do not start working until I tell you to do so."

My teacher handed out the quiz papers. I stared down at mine. So many problems. One after another after another.

I should have looked at my flashcards.

"Okay," said Ms. Colman. "You may begin the quiz . . . now!"

The first problem was $6 + 8 = $ _____. Six plus eight, six plus eight, I said to myself. Was that twelve? No, fourteen. Fourteen? I just was not sure. I began to count on my fingers. Then I noticed that the next problem was $4 + 3 = $ _____. That was

22

much easier. Four plus three equals seven. I wrote 7 in the blank. Not bad. Hannie had said not to count, and I had not counted. I went on to the third problem.

$5 + 9 =$ _____ . Five plus nine, five plus nine. I was pretty sure the answer was thirteen, so I wrote *13* in the blank. Then I went back to the first problem. I began to count on my fingers. I stopped. I peeked over at Ricky's paper. Ricky's hand was very busy. But it was busy writing, not counting. Ricky had filled in almost every blank in the first column.

So I quickly wrote *12* after $6 + 8 =$ _____ . I moved on to the fourth problem: $9 + 8 =$ _____ . I just could not answer that without counting on my fingers. I would *never* finish the quiz. I could not work fast enough.

I glanced over at Ricky's paper again. I bet his answers were almost all correct. I looked around for Ms. Colman. She was in the back of the room. She was busy with

our workbooks. I looked back at Ricky's paper. He had moved on to the second column of problems.

And then I did something I knew I should not do. I began to copy Ricky's answers onto my paper. It was wrong, but I *had* to do it. I did not want another red 68. I did not want to disappoint Ms. Colman again.

Copying certainly was faster than trying to fill in each blank by myself. When Ms. Colman said, "Time's up," I had finished all the problems in the first column and half the problems in the second column.

The Red 80

I did not sleep very well that night. I had a dream about Andrew. In the dream, the weather was sunny and hot. Except at Mommy's. The street in front of the little house was full of snow and slush. And the sky was gray. Andrew ran outside barefoot. He began to wade around in the freezing slush.

"Andrew, stop!" I yelled. "You are going to catch a cold."

"I will not!" he replied. "Anyway, I am just copying you, Karen."

After he said that, I woke up. I did not fall asleep again for a long time. (I do not know what that dream meant.)

Ms. Colman gave our quizzes back on Friday morning. I had been hoping she would wait awhile. Or maybe she would forget about them. When Hannie and Nancy and I had first arrived at school that day, we had sat on some desks in the back of the classroom. Right away, Hannie had started talking about the quizzes.

"I have been studying," she said. "Linny has been helping me with my flash cards." (Linny is Hannie's older brother.)

"But you already know your facts," I said. "You got a ninety-three."

"A ninety-three is not a one hundred," Hannie replied. "Besides, I still need to know my facts faster."

"If only Ms. Colman did not time us," I said. "That is why the quizzes are so hard. I cannot think fast enough."

"Have you looked at your flash cards?" asked Hannie.

"Well, no. Not really," I admitted. "But I think the quizzes are unfair. I hope we do not have to take anymore."

"We will," said Nancy. "Ms. Colman said so."

"Bullfrogs."

I was in a bad mood by the time school began. And then Ms. Colman handed back our quizzes. Double bullfrogs. I pouted while I waited for her to put mine on my desk. When she did, I closed my eyes. Then I opened them. At the top of the page was a big red 80.

Ms. Colman was still standing next to me. And she was smiling. "Good work, Karen," she said. "You did much better this time. You must have reviewed your facts. Keep it up."

An 80. That *was* a good grade. For a moment, I forgot how I had earned that 80. The truth is, I had not earned it at all. I had copied from Ricky. Well, mostly I had cop-

28

ied. I had filled in the first few blanks my-self, but almost all of those answers were wrong. And I had not been able to finish the quiz so those blank spaces at the end counted as wrong answers, too. The rest of the answers were really Ricky's. Only two of those were wrong.

I peeked over at Ricky's paper. Yup, he had gotten them wrong, plus a few others. At the top of *his* paper was a red 90. Ms. Colman had drawn a smiley face next to it. (She had not drawn a smiley face on my paper.)

Oh, well. At least Ms. Colman had said, "Good work, Karen," to me. She was not disappointed. And nobody except me knew I had copied from Ricky. So all I had to do was start looking at the flashcards. Then I could get an 80 by myself. Or maybe I could even get a 90 and a smiley face. It was up to me. I promised myself I would never copy from Ricky again.

At recess that day, Hannie said to Nancy and me, "I got a ninety-*four* on the second quiz. Maybe next time I will get a ninety-five."

"I got an eighty-three," said Nancy.

"What did you get, Karen?" asked Hannie.

"Let's play hopscotch," I replied.

Flash Cards

Over the weekend I really did study my flash cards. A little. I looked at them on Saturday. I looked at them again on Sunday. It was a little-house weekend at Mommy's. Not much was going on. I could concentrate better.

This is what I found out: For me, subtraction is harder than addition. And the big numbers are harder than the smaller numbers. But double numbers are easy, even if they are big. I know seven plus seven, and eight plus eight, and nine plus nine as fast as anything. But nine plus eight, or thirteen minus six . . . well, I just had not quite memorized those facts yet. I needed to count on my fingers sometimes. That's all.

I looked at my flash cards with Goosie and some of my dolls. I said to Hyacynthia, who is my best baby doll, "You are so lucky. You do not have to memorize arithmetic facts." Then I thought of something. I ran downstairs to find Mommy. I found Seth instead. "Seth?" I said. "Why do we have to memorize things like nine plus eight, and thirteen minus six? Why can't we count on our fingers?"

"Because that is too slow," Seth replied. "When you learn how to multiply and divide, you will need your facts all the time. Maybe even lots and lots of times to solve just one problem. Your work will go much faster if you have memorized your facts."

"Oh," I said. I clomped back upstairs to Hyacynthia. "Bullfrogs," I said to her. "I really do have to memorize the facts."

On Monday we did not have another quiz. I sort of forgot to look at the flash cards that night. On Tuesday we did not have a quiz either. But I thought we might have one on Wednesday. So on Tuesday night, I got out the cards. I was trying to memorize twelve minus eight, when the phone rang. A moment later, Mommy called, "Karen! It's for you!"

I put down the flash cards. I ran to the phone in Mommy's room.

"Hello?" I said. (I could hear Mommy hang up the phone in the kitchen.)

"Hi, Karen. It's me, David Michael. I have to tell you something."

"What is it?" I asked. David Michael hardly ever calls me at the little house. He must have had very big news.

David Michael whispered something into the phone.

"What? I cannot hear you," I said.

"I . . . got . . . a . . . tattoo," he said more loudly.

"You got a tattoo?" I shrieked.

34

"SHHH!" hissed my brother. "Did any-one hear you?"

"No. They are all downstairs," I told him.

"Good. Because this is a very big secret. You cannot tell *any*body."

How could David Michael have gotten a tattoo? First of all, Daddy and Elizabeth had told him not to. They had not given him permission. And second, how could my brother have let someone poke needles in him? That was gross. And probably not very safe.

"You will not tell on me, will you?" asked David Michael.

"I guess not," I said. "Where is the tattoo?"

"On my arm. Up near my shoulder. It will be hidden by my shirt sleeve. Even a T-shirt will hide it. But when I want to show it to my friends, all I have to do is roll up my sleeve."

That *was* sort of cool, I thought. "What does the tattoo look like?" I asked.

"A dragon. A green dragon."

"Awesome."

"Thanks," said David Michael. "I knew you would think so. Now do not tell on me, Karen."

"Okay," I replied. Even though I did not really want to keep the secret.

Easy as Pie

After I hung up the phone, I could not concentrate on my flashcards. All I could think about was David Michael — and the cool dragon tattoo that was a big, huge secret. So I put away the flash cards. That did not matter because on Thursday, Ms. Colman *still* did not give us another quiz.

I meant to look at the flash cards on Thursday night, but I forgot to.

On Friday, Ms. Colman said, "Boys and

girls, it is time for your third arithmetic quiz. Please clear your desks."

Well, I had not studied very much. But I had studied a little. Especially my addition facts. I knew I could solve the addition problems faster than before. And I remembered my promise. I would not copy from Ricky.

I closed my eyes for a moment. Could I get another red 80 all by myself? Yes, I said. (But what I really wanted was a red 90 and a smiley face.)

Ms. Colman was handing out the papers. When she gave me mine, I looked down at it. I saw two long columns of . . . subtraction problems: $16 - 9 = $ _____. $8 - 6 = $ _____ .

Subtraction problems? What had happened to the addition problems? Boo and bullfrogs. I was much slower at subtraction than addition.

"You may begin," said Ms. Colman, "right . . . now."

Ms. Colman checked her watch. Then she walked to the back of the room. That morning, my classmates and I had made some weather instruments for our science unit. We had also made a mess. Ms. Colman began to clean up the mess and arrange our projects. She was very busy. She was not looking at my friends and me.

Keep your eyes on your own paper, I told myself. Even so, I just *peeked* over at Ricky. His hand was moving quickly down the page.

I will not copy, I will not copy, I reminded myself. Then I remembered that I had promised myself I would not copy from *Ricky*. But I had not promised I would not copy from anyone else.

I turned my head slightly. I peeked at Natalie's paper. Natalie Springer sits on the other side of me. But I could hardly see her paper. Natalie's arm was in the way. I did notice, though, that Natalie was hard at work. And Ricky was hard at work.

I knew I should be hard at work, too.

I looked at my own paper. Okay. Sixteen minus nine. I knew I could find the correct answer if I counted on my fingers. So I did. I wrote 7 in the blank. I had answered three more problems when Ms. Colman called from the back of the room, "The quiz is half over, girls and boys. I just wanted to let you know."

Half over! I had hardly begun. If I did not answer a lot of problems fast, I would get another 68. Or something worse.

So I copied from Ricky again.

On the playground that day, Hannie and Nancy and I sat on the monkey bars. Nancy and I talked, but Hannie was very quiet.

"I think I did pretty well on the quiz today," said Nancy. "Maybe not as well as on the addition quiz, but pretty well."

"Subtraction is very hard," I said.

I looked at Hannie. She was staring across the playground.

"Hannie thought the quiz was easy, didn't you, Hannie?" said Nancy.

"Yup," replied Hannie. "As easy as pie."

"Show-off," I muttered.

Hannie glared at me. She was looking at me very strangely. Then she turned away.

The Dragon

It was another big-house weekend. On Friday, the day of the subtraction quiz, I went home to Mommy's house after school. But before suppertime, Mommy drove Andrew and me to Daddy's.

I was not in a very good mood. I felt bad about copying from Ricky again. Plus, I had left my flash cards at the little house. I wanted to study them over the weekend (since I knew Ms. Colman could give us a quiz at any time).

"Mommy," I said, as Andrew and I were getting out of the car. "I forgot my flash cards."

"Do you really need them?" she asked.

"I really do."

Mommy sighed. "All right. I will bring them over tomorrow."

"Thank you," I said. (Being a two-two is not easy.)

As soon as Andrew and I had run into the big house, David Michael pulled me upstairs. "Want to see it?" he whispered.

"See what?" I answered.

"My tattoo! Did you already forget about it?"

"Oh, sorry," I said. "Sure. Let me see it."

David Michael rolled up his sleeve. And there, by his shoulder, was a picture of a bright green dragon. It looked extra cool.

"Watch this," said David Michael. He

bent his arm back and forth, and the dragon's tail moved.

"Awesome!" I cried.

"And see? It is easy to hide. I just have to push my sleeve down."

"Yeah," I agreed. And then I said again, "Awesome."

"You could get one, too, you know."

"Who, me?" I replied. "No way." I was *not* going to get a tattoo. First of all, I did not want anyone poking me with needles. Second, I was already keeping enough secrets. I had copied from Ricky twice. I knew my brother had gotten a tattoo when he was not supposed to. I did not need a secret tattoo myself.

Later, just as my family was finishing dinner, Elizabeth said, "Well, guess what, everybody."

"What?" said Kristy.

"In two weeks the company I work for is going to have a big picnic. Everyone who works there is invited. Everyone in their families is invited, too. I hope all of you will come. This is the first time we have ever had a picnic. If people like it, we will hold one every year."

"What will we do at the picnic?" asked Charlie. "I mean, besides eat."

"You can play games and go swimming. You can spend the entire day in your bathing suits, I think," replied Elizabeth.

"Cool," said Charlie.

But I looked across the table at David Michael. This is what I wanted to say to him: "Okay, big shot. Now what are you going to do?" If he spent the day in his bathing suit, *every*one would see his tattoo.

David Michael would not look back at me. He knew he was in trouble.

Before bedtime that night, I said to my brother, "What *are* you going to do?"

"About the tattoo?" replied David Michael. "We will just have to hide it."

We will? How come I had to help David Michael with his secret?

＊　＊　＊

The weekend was awful. I did not see
Hannie at all. Every time I called her to
invite her over, she said she was too busy
to play. At least Mommy remembered to
drop off the flash cards. I studied them for
fifteen minutes on Saturday and fifteen
minutes on Sunday.

Keep Your Eyes
on Your Paper

Monday. School again. Ms. Colman took attendance. Then right away she passed back our quizzes. As soon as she started walking around the room, my heart began to pound. It sounded as if it were beating in my ears.

Thump, thump, thumpety-thump.

Finally Ms. Colman laid a paper on my desk. I looked at it quickly. At the top of the page was a red 90. (But no smiley face.) I looked over at Ricky's paper. I saw another red 90. (But no smiley face.) Then I looked at the problems I had gotten wrong. They were almost the same ones Ricky had gotten wrong. Except he had gotten the very first problem wrong, and I had gotten the very last problem wrong. (I had left that one blank because I had not been able to copy it from Ricky fast enough.)

I wondered if Ms. Colman had noticed anything about my answers and Ricky's answers.

"Boys and girls," said my teacher then, "I would like to talk to you. I want you to understand something about taking a quiz. The most important thing about it is . . . to keep your eyes on your own paper. You must do your *own* work. That is the only way we will find out what each of you has learned, and what each of you needs to work on some more. Is that clear?"

"Yes," said a couple of kids quietly.

"Sometimes," Ms. Colman went on, "you may get help when you are doing homework or a project. But when you are taking a quiz, you do your own work."

I swallowed hard. My stomach began to feel funny. Did Ms. Colman know what I had done? I could not tell. She had not said any names. Maybe someone else was copying, too.

Okay, I said to myself. Karen, you will *not* copy from Ricky anymore. You just cannot do that. It is not fair. You have to do your own work — and keep your eyes on your paper.

After I told myself that, I felt a little better. But Hannie ruined everything. She ruined it on the playground after lunch. Nancy had decided to play dodgeball with a bunch of other kids. Hannie and I were watching them. That is all we were doing. Just watching. And suddenly Hannie said to me, "I know what you did, Karen."

"What?" I said.

"I know what you did," Hannie repeated. "I saw you copy from Ricky's paper on Friday."

My stomach began to feel funny again. "I — I did not copy!" I cried.

50

"Yes, you did. Karen, I *saw* you."

"How could you see me? You sit all the way in the back of the room."

"I have very good eyesight," Hannie told me. "I can see the board from the back of the room. That is why Ms. Colman lets me sit there. I do not wear glasses like you. Anyway, I did too see you copy."

"Hannie! I am your best friend!" I exclaimed. "How could you say something like that about me?"

"Because it is true. I saw you do it."

"Liar! You did not see me do that."

"Did too."

"Did not."

Hannie did not answer. She just glared at me. So I said, "I am not talking to you anymore, Hannie Papadakis."

And she said, "Good. I do not *want* you to talk to me."

We stuck our tongues out at each other. Then I ran off to swing by myself.

100%

On Monday night, Mommy and Seth invited some friends over for dinner. They ordered two pizzas. Andrew and I got to eat with the grown-ups. I had such a good time that I forgot to look at my flash cards. I did not remember them until I was already in bed, and the light was out. Oh, well, I thought. That does not matter. I can study tomorrow night. We will not have another quiz *right* away.

Guess what. I was wrong. Ms. Colman handed out quizzes on Tuesday morning.

She handed them out first thing, as soon as she had taken attendance. While I waited for her to give me my paper, I closed my eyes. Over and over I said to myself, No subtraction, no subtraction. When I felt the paper land on my desk, I opened my eyes. An addition quiz. Whew.

"All right," said Ms. Colman a few moments later. "You may begin." Ms. Colman turned her back. She started writing on the blackboard.

I began the quiz. I answered the first two questions by myself. Then I glanced at Ricky's paper. I only wanted to see how many questions *he* had already answered. Well, for heaven's sake. He was way, *way* ahead of me. I slid my eyes over to Natalie's paper. I could not see it as well as Ricky's, but I could tell she was ahead of me, too. If I took the quiz all by myself, I would probably only answer about half the questions. I would get a horrible score. A 50%, or maybe even a 40%. How would I explain that to Ms. Colman?

I copied Ricky's entire paper.

On Thursday, Ms. Colman handed the papers back. While she was walking around the room, she said, "Class, I am proud of you. Most of you are working very hard. You are doing better and better on your quizzes. In fact, three people received one hundreds on the last quiz. They are Hannie, Ricky, and Karen."

I knew I should smile then. I knew I should look happy. But I did not *feel* happy. I had not earned that one hundred myself. Plus, Ms. Colman did not smile when she gave me my paper. And when I turned around to look at my friends, Hannie just glared at me again.

I was in a huge mess. I did not know how to get out of it.

The Three-Legged Race

The next weekend was a little-house weekend. But guess where Andrew and I went on Saturday. To the big house. This is why:

On Friday, Daddy called Mommy. He told her about Elizabeth's company picnic. He said, "I thought maybe everybody should practice for the games and special events. Tomorrow we are going to try a three-legged race and a potato sack race and an egg toss. Would Karen and Andrew like to come over? They could practice with us. We will have lots of fun. They can stay for lunch."

And that is exactly what we did.

Daddy picked up Andrew and me early in the morning. He brought us to the big house. Everyone was there. Mostly they were wearing grubby old clothes. Sam and Charlie were wearing only their swimming trunks. We gathered in the backyard.

"Okay," said Elizabeth. "The picnic is just a week away. We have to be prepared. What shall we practice first?"

"The egg toss!" shouted David Michael.

"The potato sack race," said Kristy.

"The three-legged race," said Nannie.

"Are *you* going to run in the three-legged race?" I asked Nannie.

"No," she said, "but I want to watch everyone else run in it. I might play in the egg toss, though."

"Let's try the three-legged race," said Elizabeth.

"How do we do it?" asked Andrew.

"Like this," said Daddy. "Andrew, why don't you and Karen be partners. Come stand in front of me."

Andrew and I stood next to each other. Daddy tied my right leg to Andrew's left leg. We were supposed to run together! We ran for four steps and fell down. *Thud!* Everyone laughed. Then *they* wanted to try the three-legged race.

All morning long we practiced. We ran around with our legs tied together. We hopped in potato sacks. We tossed eggs back and forth. (They were hard-boiled, in case they broke.) The weather grew hotter and hotter. Kristy put on her bathing suit. Then Andrew and I changed into our suits.

"David Michael?" said Elizabeth. "Don't you want to put on your swimming trunks?"

"No. That's all right," replied my brother.

Elizabeth looked at him strangely, so I poked him. But David Michael just said, "Come on, everybody. Let's try the three-legged race again."

"What is a three-legged race?" someone asked.

I looked up. Hannie had come into the yard. She was watching us.

"Hi, Hannie!" called Kristy. "How are you? I have not seen you in awhile."

"I'm fine," said Hannie. (She did not say that she and I were mad at each other.)

"How is school going?" asked Kristy.

"Fine," said Hannie again. "I got a one hundred on an arithmetic quiz." She paused. Then she added, "So did Karen."

"Karen!" exclaimed Daddy. "You got a one hundred on a math quiz? Why didn't you tell us? That is fantastic!"

"Um, thanks," I said. I tried to smile. I knew I should look proud.

"What was the quiz on?" asked Nannie.

"Addition," I said.

"Will you show us your paper?" Elizabeth wanted to know.

"I can't. I left it at school." I turned around and stuck my tongue out at Hannie. Then I said, "Okay. Let's practice some more."

Emily's Tattoo

By lunchtime, everyone in my big-house family was tired from our practicing. We took a break and ate sandwiches in the backyard. We rested for awhile. Then we practiced some more. David Michael and I were getting pretty good at jumping around in sacks. We were not bad at tossing eggs, either.

At three o'clock, Emily fell and bumped her chin.

Then Sam said he had a headache.

"Time to stop practicing," said Elizabeth.

We went inside to cool off. We had been sitting in the kitchen with glasses of water, when Daddy said, "Where are Emily and Andrew?"

"I will look for them," replied Kristy. "Come on, Karen."

Kristy and I found Emily and Andrew upstairs in the playroom.

"Oh, no!" cried Kristy, when she saw them. "What are you *do*ing?"

"We have tattoos," said Andrew proudly.

"Tattoos," repeated Emily.

"We drew them ourselves," added Andrew. "We did not have to go to a tattoo parlor."

Emily and Andrew were covered with little Magic Marker drawings.

"Look," said Andrew. "I made a whale here, and a turtle here, and over here are Rocky and Midgie."

"I make cat!" exclaimed Emily. She pointed to a purple blob on her knee. "Boo-Boo cat. All by myself."

62

"Oh, brother," said Kristy. "Now where did you get the idea to give yourselves tattoos? Come on, you guys. Let me clean you up."

Kristy took Emily and Andrew into the bathroom. And I ran downstairs and found David Michael. "I have to talk to you," I hissed. I made him come outside with me.

"What is it?" he asked crossly.

"Emily and Andrew gave themselves tattoos with Magic Markers. They must have seen your dragon. I do not want to keep your secret anymore. You have to tell your mother what you did."

"No way," said my brother. (He did not sound very worried.)

"Okay-ay," I sang. "But you will be sorry."

"You are a worry wart," replied David Michael.

And that was that.

Ricky's Cold

On Sunday, I looked at my flash cards. I quizzed myself. I decided that maybe I knew my addition facts a little faster. Even so, when I went to school on Monday, I was not feeling very happy. I knew that copying from Ricky was wrong. Plus, Hannie was still mad at me, and Nancy wanted to know why, but Hannie and I would not tell her. Also, Daddy wanted me to bring home the quiz with the red 100% on top. My big mess was getting bigger and bigger.

When Ms. Colman came into the room, she took attendance. "Where is Ricky today?" she asked us.

Bobby Gianelli raised his hand. "At home with a cold," he replied. "I talked to him yesterday. He will be back tomorrow."

Poor Ricky, I thought. Too bad he has to stay at home on a nice day like today.

After that, I did not think much about Ricky. Not until the afternoon. That was when Ms. Colman said, "Time for the next quiz, boys and girls."

My heart beat faster. I looked down at the paper Ms. Colman laid on my desk. It was full of subtraction problems. What was I going to do? I could not take that quiz. I had just realized something awful. I *needed* to copy from Ricky. If I did not copy, I would probably not finish half the test. Then what would I say to Ms. Colman? Or to Daddy or Mommy or Seth or Elizabeth? Or to Hannie, who had already seen me copying from Ricky?

I could feel my heart pounding in my ears

again. I watched Ms. Colman. She had returned to the front of the room. I knew she was about to say, "You may begin the quiz." So before she could do that, I raised my hand.

"Yes, Karen?" said Ms. Colman.

"I do not feel very well," I told her. "May I go to the nurse?"

Ms. Colman paused. Then she said, "What's the matter?"

"Um, my stomach is upset."

"Are you sure you need to go to the nurse?"

"Yes," I answered. "I think I might throw up." (I knew no one would want me to barf in our classroom.)

Sure enough, Pamela Harding said, "Ew, gross."

"All right," said Ms. Colman. "Natalie, will you walk Karen to the nurse, please? Then come right back so you can begin the quiz."

Natalie walked me down the hall to the nurse's office. When she left me there, she

called over her shoulder, "I hope you do not barf, Karen!"

"Thank you," I replied politely. (My stomach felt just fine.)

"Well, Karen," said the nurse. "What seems to be the problem?"

"My stomach is a little upset. Could I lie down for awhile?"

Our nurse is Mrs. Pazden, and she is very nice. Her office smells kind of funny, though. Actually, so does Mrs. Pazden. But that was okay. The smells are just medicines and Band-Aids.

Mrs. Pazden led me to the cot. It is in a dark corner of the room, in case anyone needs to go to sleep. I lay down on the cot.

I stayed there until Mrs. Pazden said, "School is almost over now, Karen. Do you think you can walk back to your classroom?"

"Yes," I replied. I stood up — but not too fast. After all, I was supposed to be sick. I walked through the hallway to Ms. Colman's room. My classmates were getting ready to leave. They were taking things out of their desks and lining up at the door. I lined up with them.

"Do you feel better now?" Ms. Colman asked me.

"Yes, thank you," I said. I let out a sigh. The subtraction quiz was over. I had not had to take it.

15

Karen's Big Lie

Ricky came back to school on Tuesday, just as Bobby had said he would.

"How do you feel?" Ms. Colman asked him.

"Fine, thanks," he replied. "My cold is all gone."

"We had another arithmetic quiz yesterday," Ms. Colman told him. "I would like for you to make it up. I will give it to you right after lunch. You will miss the beginning of recess, but after you are finished you may go outside."

"Okay," said Ricky. "I am ready." (At least he did not say the quiz would be as easy as pie.)

"Karen, you missed the quiz, too," Ms. Colman went on. "I would like for you to make it up with Ricky."

Make it *up*? But I had not been *absent*. I had just missed the quiz. Oh, well. Maybe when lunch was over, I could pretend I had forgotten about the quiz. I would just go out to the playground.

Ms. Colman did not let me forget. She came into the cafeteria during lunchtime. She waited for Ricky and me to finish eating. Then she led us back to our classroom. We sat at our desks. Ms. Colman gave us the sheets of subtraction problems.

And then she sat down at her desk. She was right in front of us. "You may begin," she said. She did not move.

Uh-oh. How could I peek at Ricky's paper? Ms. Colman would see me. So I solved the first problem by myself.

Knock, knock, knock. Mr. Berger was leaning in our doorway. His classroom is next to ours. He called Ms. Colman into the hall. They stood outside and talked.

While they talked, I copied Ricky's quiz. I was getting pretty good at sliding my eyes over to his paper. Ricky did not know what I was doing. I wrote busily, almost as fast as Ricky.

By the time Ms. Colman came back, we were nearly finished with the quiz. I had to solve the last two problems by myself. Luckily, they were easy ones. They were $10 - 2 = $ _____ and $8 - 5 = $ _____.

"Time's up," said Ms. Colman, just as I was writing 3 in the blank.

"Can I go outside now?" asked Ricky. "Please?"

"I think I will correct your quizzes first," replied Ms. Colman.

She corrected them quickly. When she was finished, she said, "Well, this is very interesting."

"What is?" I asked. (I could feel butter-flies in my tummy.)

"You both got eighty-eights."

Ricky looked confused. "That is not bad, is it?" he asked.

"Oh, no. It is a very good score," said Ms. Colman. "But you and Karen both missed the same problems. The exact same ones."

"Probably the hardest ones," said Ricky.

"And you both came up with the same wrong answers."

Ricky frowned. He looked at me. I looked down at my desk.

"Ricky, please come here," said Ms. Colman. She was sitting behind her desk. She talked to Ricky for a few minutes. Then she let him go outside for the rest of recess. After that she sat down at her desk again. "Karen," she said, "you and Ricky have been getting a lot of the same wrong answers lately. That is very strange. Do you want to tell me anything about it?" (I shook my head.) "I asked Ricky if he has been

74

copying from you. He said no. So now I will ask you something. Have you been copying from Ricky?"

"No," I replied.

I had just told my teacher a big lie.

The Stay-at-Home Day

I knew I had done a very bad thing. In fact, I had done several bad things. I had been copying from Ricky's quizzes. (That is cheating.) I had been helping David Michael keep a naughty secret. I had faked a stomachache. I had lied to Hannie. But worst of all, I had lied to Ms. Colman, my best teacher ever. My big mess was a big problem. And I did not know what to do about it.

When I came home from school on the day I lied to Ms. Colman, I went straight to my room. I stayed there until supper-time. At suppertime I sat in the kitchen with Mommy and Seth and Andrew, but I could hardly eat.

"What is wrong?" Seth asked me.

"Do you feel all right, honey?" Mommy asked me.

"Are you going to throw up?" Andrew asked me.

"I'm okay," I said.

But I did not eat much dinner. Afterward, I looked at my flash cards for awhile, and then I just went to bed early. But I woke up early, too. I woke up long before anyone else in the house did, even the pets. I lay in bed and thought about my big mess. I decided I was a bad person. How could I ever look at Ms. Colman again? How could I look her in the eye, knowing I had told her such an awful lie? How could I be the flower girl in her wedding? I was in T-R-O-U-B-L-E.

By the time Mommy woke up, I really did not feel very well. I even thought I might barf. So I said to Mommy, "Could I stay home from school today?"

Mommy put her hand on my forehead. "You do not have a fever," she replied.

"But I still do not feel well. Andrew was right. I might throw up."

"Well . . ." said Mommy. "Are you *sure* you are sick enough to stay home?"

"Yes." I nodded my head.

"All right. Get back in bed then. I will bring you some tea and toast."

"No, thank you. I cannot eat."

I climbed into bed. Later, Seth came in to say good-bye. He kissed my forehead. "Feel better, Karen," he said. "I am going to work now. I will see you tonight. I will bring you a little present."

I tried to smile, but I could not. "That is okay. You do not have to bring me a present," I said. (I knew I did not deserve one.)

The morning seemed long. Andrew left for preschool. (His car pool picked him up.) Mommy worked at her desk downstairs. I looked at my books by Mr. Roald Dahl —

Matilda and *The Witches* and *Charlie and the Chocolate Factory* and *James and the Giant Peach*. I had gotten them for my seventh birthday. I decided I was glad that when I turned seven, I did not know what a hard time I would have *being* seven.

I was just starting to feel bored when Mommy called to me. "Karen?" she said. "Do you think you could eat a little lunch?"

"I do not know," I said. (That was the truth.)

"Well, come downstairs for awhile and talk to me."

So I did. Mommy and I sat at the table in the kitchen. I ate some crackers and drank some juice.

"Honey," said Mommy, "I am worried about you. So are Daddy and Seth and Elizabeth. You have not seemed like yourself. Is anything wrong? Are you having trouble in school?" (I thought about what to answer. I did not want to tell another lie.) "We want you to know we are very proud of you," Mommy went on. "You have been working hard lately. Especially in math. I know math is not easy for you. And your quiz scores have been excellent."

I almost told Mommy how I had *really* earned those quiz scores. But Andrew came home then, and he wanted lunch. So I did not say anything.

Prizes

"Hi, honey. How are you feeling?" said Mommy when she woke me the next morning. "Is your tummy better?"

"I guess so," I replied.

"Good. Back to school then."

"Okay."

I got dressed for school. I wondered if I had missed another quiz when I had been absent. But I did not really care. If I had missed one, I knew I would have to make it up.

In school, Ms. Colman started talking about those darn old quizzes right away. As soon as she had closed her attendance book, she said, "Girls and boys, I have an announcement."

Usually Ms. Colman makes Surprising Announcements, which I like very much. But on that day, I did not care about annoucements at all. Not until Ms. Colman began to speak.

"As you know," my teacher said, "all the students at Stoneybrook Academy have been taking math quizzes for several weeks now. Yesterday, your principal decided that the next quiz will be a contest. In each class, the two students who receive the highest scores will get — "

"A trip to Disney World?" guessed Bobby.

Everyone laughed, even Ms. Colman.

"No," said Ms. Colman. (She was still smiling.) "Each one will get a coupon for a free ice-cream sundae at the Rosebud Cafe."

"Yea!" cheered my classmates.

But all I said was, "When do we take the next quiz?"

"Right now," replied Ms. Colman.

"Oh." I had had a feeling she would say that.

Ms. Colman scooped a stack of papers off her desk. She walked up and down the rows, handing a quiz to each of us. When she gave me mine, I did not even look at it. I did not care whether it was an addition quiz or a subtraction quiz.

That was because I had made a decision. I could not copy from Ricky's paper again. I already felt horrible. But I would feel much, much worse if I got a free ice-cream sundae that someone else should have won.

I knew I would not do well on the quiz, though. And later I would have to explain that to Ms. Colman.

I sighed loudly. Then I looked down at my paper.

It was a subtraction quiz.

"Okay, class. You may begin," said Ms. Colman.

Keep your eyes on your paper, I told myself. And I did. I did not let them slide to the left to look at Ricky's quiz. I did not let them slide to the right to try to peek at Natalie's quiz. I just stared down at the first problem: $19 - 8 =$ _____. That would take lots of counting. But I counted anyway.

Eighteen, seventeen, sixteen, fifteen, fourteen, thirteen, twelve, eleven. Nineteen minus eight equals eleven. I wrote *11* in the blank.

I went on to the next problem: $9 - 5 =$ _____. That was easy. I knew that problem by heart. I wrote *4* in the blank. But the next problem was $16 - 7 =$ _____. I had to count again.

Slowly, slowly I worked on the quiz. When Ms. Colman said, "Time's up," I had not even finished the first column of prob-

lems. I looked at Ricky's paper. He had finished every one. There was nothing I could do. I handed in my quiz along with the others.

It was time to talk to Ms. Colman.

The Truth

I did not get to talk to Ms. Colman until lunchtime. After she collected our quizzes, she put them in a pile on her desk. Then she took us to the library for story hour. After that, we worked on our weather instruments. And after that came lunchtime.

"Please line up at the door," said Ms. Colman.

I stood up very slowly so I could be the last person on line. Pamela was at the head of the line. She led our class past Ms. Colman and down the hall. (Sometimes we are allowed to walk to the cafeteria by our-selves.) But I did not go out the door. When I reached Ms. Colman, I said, "May I talk to you, please?"

"Of course," replied my teacher.

Ms. Colman sat at her desk and I sat across from her at mine.

"I have to tell you something," I said. "I have been copying from Ricky when we take our quizzes. That is why I have been doing so well. I know I should not copy, but the quizzes are so *hard*. I cannot work fast enough. I still count on my fingers."

I told Ms. Colman the whole story — everything I had done, and all my secrets. I even told her about the fight with Hannie and about David Michael's tattoo. I said I hoped Ms. Colman still wanted me to be her flower girl. By the time I finished, I was crying.

Ms. Colman stood up then. She walked around to my desk and put her arm across my shoulders. "I am glad you told me the truth, Karen," she said. "And I'm sorry you have had such a hard time. I want you to understand something, though. When you cheat, who do you hurt the most?" She looked at me very seriously.

"Myself," I whispered.

"And what happens when you lie?"

"You have to tell bigger and bigger lies. It never ends!" I exclaimed.

"That's right. Karen, I also want you to remember something," Ms. Colman went on. "You are the youngest student in this class. You have skipped a grade. You skipped because you are very smart. But do not expect *every*thing to be easy for you."

"All right," I said. (I was feeling gigundoly better.) "When I go home today," I added, "I will tell Mommy what I did. I will call Daddy and tell him, too."

"Good for you," said Ms. Colman. "I will also call your parents. And Karen, of course I still want you to be my flower girl."

I talked to Mommy as soon as I came home from school. I told her almost everything. (I did not tell her about the tattoo.

That was a big-house problem.) Mommy looked as serious as Ms. Colman had looked.

Guess what. Ms. Colman telephoned while Mommy and I were still talking. They had a very long conversation. When they hung up, Mommy said she wanted to talk to Seth when he came home from work.

I spent the afternoon looking at my flash-cards. Finally I called Daddy at the big house. (I had to wait until he came home from work.) I told *him* what I had done. Then I said I wanted to talk to Elizabeth, too. When she picked up the phone, I said, "Daddy, Elizabeth, I do not want to keep bad secrets ever again. So I have to tell you what David Michael did. I am sorry if this is tattling, but I think you should know that David Michael got a tattoo. He did it even after you told him not to."

"What?" cried Daddy and Elizabeth.

Then Elizabeth dropped the phone and went looking for my brother. "You will not believe this," she said when she came back.

"David Michael did get a tattoo. But not a real one. He did not go to a tattoo parlor. He rubbed a temporary tattoo on his arm. He showed me where it was. He barely washed that arm for weeks. Even so, the tattoo finally faded away. It is gone now."

More Truth

I wished my problems were gone like David Michael's tattoo. But they were not. In fact, the only thing I did not get in trouble for was telling on David Michael. Daddy and Elizabeth said they understood why I had done that. They said nobody should have to keep bad secrets. (I think David Michael got in an intsy bit of trouble for putting on the fake tattoo when he was not supposed to get *any* tattoo.)

But Mommy and Seth said I needed a

punishment for cheating and lying. Daddy and Elizabeth said the same thing. And Ms. Colman said I needed extra math help.

Boo and bullfrogs.

I knew they were right, though. I also knew I had to tell the truth to two more people. Hannie and Ricky. Plus, I needed to apologize to them. I had lied to Hannie, and I had almost gotten Ricky in trouble. (I could not believe how big my mess had become.)

These were my punishments: Mommy and Seth said no TV for two entire weeks. Daddy and Elizabeth said no allowance for two weeks. Then Ms. Colman suggested that since I would not be watching TV, I could study my flash cards instead. I was supposed to study them each day with a grown-up.

The day after I told the truth to Ms. Colman was a Friday. I asked Seth if he could take me to school a few minutes early. I wanted to have time to talk to Ricky. When Seth dropped me off at Stoneybrook Academy, I went straight to my classroom. I waited for Ricky.

As soon as I saw him, I said, "Ricky, could I talk to you, please? In private? It is important."

"Okay," replied Ricky (even though he wanted to play Kleenex tag with Bobby and Hank).

I led Ricky to the back of the room. We stood by the sink. "Ricky," I said, "I have to tell you something. I have been copying your math quizzes. Ms. Colman knows about it. I told her yesterday."

"You *copied*?" exclaimed Ricky. "From *my* papers? How many times?"

"Well, a lot," I admitted.

"So that is why we kept getting the same grades," said Ricky. "No fair, Karen! You know, Ms. Colman thought *I* was cheating."

"Not anymore. She knows the truth."

"Boy," said Ricky. He shook his head. "How am I supposed to trust you now? Are you going to copy from me again?"

"Never," I answered. "Never ever. I promise."

"Okay. Then I forgive you. After all, you are my wife."

Ricky and Bobby and Hank started their game of Kleenex tag then. (It is a very silly, made-up game.) I waited for Hannie to come in. I wanted to talk to her next. But by the time Ms. Colman was taking attendance, Hannie had still not arrived.

"She has a cold," Nancy said. "I talked to her last night."

(I heard Pamela whisper to Leslie, "I bet she caught it from Ricky.")

"Oh, that is too bad," said Ms. Colman. "Because I have good news for her. And for someone else in this room. I would like to announce the winners of the ice-cream sundaes. They are Ricky and Hannie. Congratulations to both of you." Ms. Colman gave Ricky his coupon.

I raised my hand then. "Ms. Colman?" I said. "If you want, I could give Hannie her coupon. I will be seeing her this weekend." (I did not add that I would be seeing her because I had to say a very big "I'm sorry" to my best friend.)

The Picnic

I was standing on Hannie's doorstep. It was Friday afternoon. Mommy had just taken Andrew and me to Daddy's. We were there for a big-house weekend. And the next day we would go to Elizabeth's company picnic.

I waited nervously for someone to answer the door. In my hand was Hannie's coupon. In my mind was an invitation for her.

The door opened. Hannie stood in front of me.

"Karen!" she exclaimed.

"Hi. How are you feeling?"

"Better. I think I will be all well tomorrow."

"That's good. I have something for you." I held out the coupon. "It is from Ms. Colman. You won a free ice-cream sundae at the Rosebud Cafe. So did Ricky. I told Ms. Colman I would give this to you."

"Thanks," said Hannie. She took the coupon.

"Hannie, could I come in, please? I need to talk to you."

Hannie let out this gigundo sigh. But she did let me in. We went to her room. We sat on her bed.

"Okay," I began. "You were right, Hannie. I did copy from Ricky. I copied lots of times. Ms. Colman knows now. So do my parents. I told them yesterday. I got in a lot of trouble. And I apologized to Ricky this morning. Now I want to apologize to you. I am sorry I copied. I am sorry I lied to you. And I am very, very sorry we had a fight."

Hannie glanced at me. "Is our fight over?" she asked.

"I hope so," I replied.

"Oh, good," said Hannie. "I missed talking to you."

"And I missed talking to you. . . . Hannie? If you knew I was copying from Ricky, why didn't you tell Ms. Colman?"

Hannie shrugged. "I don't know. I guess I wanted you to do it yourself. But if you had not done that soon, I probably *would* have told on you. I am glad *you* told, though."

"Yeah," I agreed. "I got into a huge mess, but I learned my lesson. I learned lots of lessons." I stood up. It was time to go home for supper. Then I remembered something. "Hey, Hannie, guess what. Tomorrow my big-house family is going to a huge picnic. Daddy and Elizabeth said I could invite you. Do you want to come with us?"

"Sure!" exclaimed Hannie. "Just let me check with my parents."

I have never seen so much food in my life. Except maybe at a grocery store. This is what was served at the picnic on Saturday — hamburgers, hot dogs, chicken, fruit salad, regular salad, deviled eggs, pie, and ice cream. The food was spread out on long tables.

We did not eat right away. We played games first.

Hannie and I tied our legs together for the three-legged race. We ran five steps before we fell down. Andrew and David Michael were behind us. They fell on top of us.

"Yikes!" cried Hannie. (We were all laughing.)

"Boy, is it hot today," said David Michael as we tried to stand up. He pulled off his shirt.

"Hey, show Hannie your —" I started to say. I peered at David Michael's shoulder.

"Where is the dragon?" I asked him.

"All gone," he replied.

"So it really did fade away."

"Yup."

"Are you going to put on another?"

"No way," said my brother. "The dragon was cool, but I did not like keeping him a secret. Some secrets are no fun."

"You're not kidding," I said. Then I turned to Hannie. "Come on! They are going to start the potato sack race. Let's go!"

I took Hannie's hand, and we ran across the grass together.

About the Author

ANN M. MARTIN lives in New York City and loves animals, especially cats. She has two cats of her own, Mouse and Rosie.

Other books by Ann M. Martin that you might enjoy are *Stage Fright*; *Me and Katie (the Pest)*; and the books in *The Baby-sitters Club* series.

Ann likes ice cream and *I Love Lucy*. And she has her own little sister, whose name is Jane.

Little Sister

Don't miss #39

KAREN'S WEDDING

When I woke up the next morning, I realized I had butterflies in my stomach. It was wedding day, and I was an intsy bit nervous.

I peeked outside. I saw sunshine and a blue sky.

I tried to eat breakfast that morning, but it was hard.

"Eat *some*thing," said Seth. "It is a long time until lunch."

So I ate a piece of toast. Then I ran back to my room. I could not wait to get dressed. I put on my underwear. I put on a pair of white tights. I put on the dress and my shoes and the gloves. Then I took off the gloves so I could fix my hair. After that I put the gloves back on, and then the hat. "I'm ready!" I shouted.

LITTLE APPLE

BABY-SITTERS

Little Sister®

by Ann M. Martin, author of *The Baby-sitters Club*®

❑	MQ44300-3	#1	Karen's Witch	$2.75
❑	MQ44259-7	#2	Karen's Roller Skates	$2.75
❑	MQ44299-7	#3	Karen's Worst Day	$2.75
❑	MQ44264-3	#4	Karen's Kittycat Club	$2.75
❑	MQ44258-9	#5	Karen's School Picture	$2.75
❑	MQ43651-1	#10	Karen's Grandmothers	$2.75
❑	MQ43650-3	#11	Karen's Prize	$2.75
❑	MQ43649-X	#12	Karen's Ghost	$2.75
❑	MQ43648-1	#13	Karen's Surprise	$2.75
❑	MQ43646-5	#14	Karen's New Year	$2.75
❑	MQ43645-7	#15	Karen's in Love	$2.75
❑	MQ43644-9	#16	Karen's Goldfish	$2.75
❑	MQ43643-0	#17	Karen's Brothers	$2.75
❑	MQ43642-2	#18	Karen's Home-Run	$2.75
❑	MQ43641-4	#19	Karen's Good-Bye	$2.95
❑	MQ44823-4	#20	Karen's Carnival	$2.75
❑	MQ44824-2	#21	Karen's New Teacher	$2.95
❑	MQ44833-1	#22	Karen's Little Witch	$2.95
❑	MQ44832-3	#23	Karen's Doll	$2.95
❑	MQ44859-5	#24	Karen's School Trip	$2.75
❑	MQ44831-5	#25	Karen's Pen Pal	$2.75
❑	MQ44830-7	#26	Karen's Ducklings	$2.75
❑	MQ44829-3	#27	Karen's Big Joke	$2.75
❑	MQ44828-5	#28	Karen's Tea Party	$2.75
❑	MQ44825-0	#29	Karen's Cartwheel	$2.75
❑	MQ45645-8	#30	Karen's Kittens	$2.75
❑	MQ45646-6	#31	Karen's Bully	$2.95
❑	MQ45647-4	#32	Karen's Pumpkin Patch	$2.95
❑	MQ45648-2	#33	Karen's Secret	$2.95
❑	MQ45650-4	#34	Karen's Snow Day	$2.95
❑	MQ45652-0	#35	Karen's Doll Hosital	$2.95